SURA'S

BIRBAL AND HIS CLEVERNESS

By
Neela Subramaniam

SURA BOOKS (Pvt) LTD.

Chennai ● Bangalore ● Kolkata ● Ernakulam

Price: Rs.25.00

© PUBLISHERS

Birbal and his Cleverness

by Neela Subramaniam

First Edition : June, 2006

Size : ⅛ Crown

Pages : 48

Price: Rs.25.00

ISBN: 81-7478-821-2

SURA BOOKS (PVT) LTD.

Head Office:
1620, 'J' Block,
16th Main Road,
Anna Nagar,
Chennai - 600040.
Phones: 26162173, 26161099.

Branch:
XXXII/2328, New Kalavath Road,
Opp. to BSNL, Near Chennoth Glass,
Palarivattom,
Ernakulam - 682025.
Phone: 0484-3205797

Printed at T. Krishna Press, Chennai - 600 102 and Published by V.V.K.Subburaj for Sura Books (Pvt) Ltd., 1620, 'J' Block, 16th Main Road, Anna Nagar, Chennai - 600 040. Phones: 26162173, 26161099. Fax: (91) 44-26162173. email: surabooks@eth.net website: www.surabooks.com

Contents

A

Contents

(iii)

STORIES OF BIRBAL'S CLEVERNESS

1. THE LOYAL SERVANT

One day, the Emperor Akbar was out strolling with Birbal in the palace garden. Suddenly he began praising the Brinjal.

"Brinjal is a very tasty vegetable. It is also good for the body", Akbar said.

"You are right, O Badshah! Brinjal is indeed a very tasty vegetable. There is no other vegetable which is better than the brinjal!" Birbal agreed at once.

"Aha! Now I have the chance to test Birbal!" Akbar thought to himself.

Some days later, Akbar ordered brinjals to be cooked in the royal kitchen. When the dish of brinjals was served to the Emperor, he said, "No, I don't want it. I don't like brinjals. They are full of seeds and are not good for the body. Give the dish to Birbal, he is very fond of brinjals."

The dish was offered to Birbal. But he too did not want it.

"I hate brinjals. It is not good", he said.

Akbar was surprised to hear Birbal's remark.

"What is this, Birbal? The other day you praised the brinjal and said that there was no better vegetable than the brinjal!" he exclaimed.

"O Badshah! I am your servant, but not the brinjal's. You can make me a Minister and give me rich rewards, but the brinjal can't" - Birbal pointed out.

The cleverness of Birbal's reply increased Akbar's opinion of his able Minister.

❊❊ ❊❊ ❊❊

2. BIRBAL FREES THE LION

The Emperor Akbar was friendly with other rulers of his time, especially with the Emperor of Persia. The two Emperors often sent puzzles and riddles for each to solve. It was a battle of wits.

Once, the Emperor of Persia sent a lion in a cage to the Emperor Akbar. The huge lion looked so lifelike that many people were fooled into thinking that it was a real animal.

The messengers who brought the gift said to Akbar, "O Badshah! Our Emperor has asked you to solve the following riddle: Take the lion out of the cage without breaking the cage or disturbing the lion's position using physical forces. Our Emperor has given 3 weeks for you to solve the riddle."

They bowed and left the court.

Akbar was at a loss. He did not know what the riddle meant.

"Can anyone help?" he looked at his courtiers and asked.

They shook their heads. For, solving the riddle seemed to be almost impossible.

Akbar missed Birbal greatly. Birbal had gone on a pilgrimage to holy places and could not be reached

quickly. Akbar was also troubled because if he could not solve the riddle, he would become a laughing stock. So, he tried to think of all the ways to release the lion from the cage.

To Akbar's surprise and greater delight, Birbal returned unexpectedly. Due to his wife's ill health, he could not travel very far. Birbal went to the palace when he received Akbar's message.

Akbar showed the lion in the cage and read out the Persian Emperor's riddle.

Birbal walked all round the cage and looked at the lion closely.

"Please can you give me a day's time to solve the riddle?" he asked.

Akbar looked happier than before. He knew that Birbal would succeed somehow in solving the riddle.

Birbal examined the lion again. He noted that it looked as if it was made of some kind of metal. But he thought that the beast's feet were oddly made. Birbal put his hand through the bars and touched them. At once he realised what to do!

"Aha! The lion is really made of wax and has been coated with metallic paint", he thought.

The next day, Birbal came to court carrying a long and thick iron rod. He asked one of the guards to heat the rod's end till it became red-hot. When the rod was hot enough to his satisfaction, Birbal took

it in his hand and walked to the lion's cage. He stood very near, and inserted the rod into the cage. To everyone's surprise, the lion began melting. Within a short time, the lion had vanished from the cage. It was empty now.

The riddle had been solved! Everyone clapped loudly and the prestige of the Moghul Empire had also been saved. Akbar embraced Birbal gratefully and rewarded him with costly gifts.

❉❉   ❉❉   ❉❉

3. THE WARMTH OF LIGHT

It was a cold day in winter. Akbar was strolling along the banks of the River Yamuna with Birbal. A thought occurred to him as he gazed at the water.

"I want to know if anyone in this city can stand up to his neck in the icy water of the Yamuna for a whole night", Akbar said. "I will give 200 silver coins to anyone who can perform the deed."

Birbal asked messengers to pass the Emperor's challenge to all the people in the city.

Not many people dared to take up the challenge. But there was a poor man who badly needed the money. He came to the palace and told Akbar that he would stand in the cold waters of the Yamuna for an entire night.

Akbar at once made two guards watch the man all the time. When the next day dawned, the guards took the poor man to the Emperor.

"So you have passed my test successfully! Guards, did he stand in the water up to his neck?" Akbar asked.

"Yes, O Badshah", they replied respectfully.

"Tell me, did you have anything to help you while you were standing all night in the cold water?" Akbar asked the poor man.

"I stood in the cold water looking at the lamps lit in the towers of the palace and imagined its warmth", he replied.

"Then you have cheated! I cannot give you the reward. So, go away!" Akbar exclaimed.

The poor man was surprised to hear the Emperor's words. But he dared not argue. So, he went away sadly. He remembered Birbal.

"I will ask Raja Birbal to help me", he decided and went to see Birbal.

The poor man told Birbal the entire story.

"Don't worry! I shall see that the Emperor gives you your reward", Birbal said and sent the man away.

Akbar decided to go hunting the next morning. He sent a messenger to ask Birbal to accompany him. The man came back after some time.

"Raja Birbal asked me to tell you that he is cooking 'Khitchdi' and will come after he has finished" - the messenger said to Akbar.

Akbar waited for some more time. But Birbal still did not come.

"How much longer will I have to wait! I will go and see what wonderful dish Birbal is cooking and then go off hunting if he can't come with me", Akbar said and set out for Birbal's mansion.

He stopped and stared with surprise when he reached the courtyard of Birbal's mansion. Birbal had lit a small fire. From the overhanging branch of a tree hung a pot.

"What, Birbal! Is this the way to cook 'khitchdi'? How can this small fire heat the pot which is far away?" Akbar made fun of Birbal.

"It can happen, O Badshah! Just as the far away lamps of the palace can give warmth to a man standing in the cold waters of the Yamuna river!" Birbal replied.

At once Akbar remembered his words to the poor man. He told his guards to fetch the poor man at once.

"Thank you, Birbal, for making me see the injustice of my action", Akbar said to Birbal as they returned to the palace.

He rewarded the poor man with the 200 silver coins and gave him other gifts too.

❈❈   ❈❈   ❈❈

4. BIRBAL AND AKBAR'S PARROT

Once, the Emperor Akbar was presented with a beautiful parrot by one of his subjects. The parrot had been trained to talk and sing. Akbar was very pleased to receive such a bird. He kept it in a special cage made of gold. Akbar appointed two servants to look after the parrot.

"It is your special duty to look after the parrot day and night. The person who comes to me and says that it is dead, will face the death sentence" - Akbar warned them.

The two servants faithfully looked after the parrot. They fed it regularly with good food and kept its cage clean so that the Emperor would be pleased. The men spent so much time in looking after the parrot, that they themselves grew thin and weak. But they still did not want any harm to come to the parrot.

One night, in spite of their efforts to stay awake, the men fell asleep. They woke up in the morning and saw the parrot lying lifeless in the golden cage.

The two servants trembled with fear. They dared not to tell the Emperor about the parrot's death. He had warned that the man who informed him about

the parrot's death, would meet with the death sentence. So the two servants wondered what to do.

"I have an idea! Let us go to see the wise Raja Birbal. He will surely help us", one of them said.

They both went to Birbal's mansion and told him all about the parrot and also about Akbar's warning.

"Please save us somehow! If you can't save us, no one in this world can!" they begged.

"Leave everything to me, and don't worry! I will look after the matter and talk to the Emperor myself." Birbal said and sent them away.

Birbal went to see the Emperor Akbar.

"O Badshah! I have some strange news for you. Your parrot is not talking or singing. Its eyes are closed and it is lying still without moving. Can it be meditating?" Birbal wondered.

"What! Is my parrot dead?" Akbar exclaimed. "I must see with my own eyes."

Birbal went with Akbar to the room where the parrot's golden cage had been kept.

"Look, my parrot is dead!" Akbar cried.

"What you say is true", Birbal agreed. Then he reminded Akbar about his warning to the two servants. "You told them that they would be punished

with death if they reported to you about the parrot's death. So they did not tell you. They came to me for help. I too did not tell you that the parrot was dead. You said it yourself!"

The Emperor knew that he should not have said such a thing to his innocent servants. They could not help it if the bird died.

"Thank you for pointing out my mistake, Birbal" - Akbar said.

❋   ❋   ❋

5. POETIC JUSTICE

In the city of Agra, there lived a man. Though he was very rich, he was extremely a stingy. Many people came to his house hoping that he would help them. But the rich man never gave anything to anyone. He managed to keep them in good-humour and sent them away with false promises.

One day, a young poet called Raidas came to the rich man's house. He was welcomed warmly by the rich man who asked, "What can I do for you?"

"I have composed many poems. I would like to read them out to you", replied Raidas.

"How wonderful! I like poetry very much. So, please read them to me", said the rich man.

He listened with great interest to Raidas' poems. The rich man particularly liked the poem in which Raidas had compared him to Kubera, the God of Wealth.

"I am very pleased with your poems. I wish to reward you for your talent. Please come tomorrow to accept the gifts", said the rich man.

Raidas was very happy. He nodded his head and went away. But when he came to the house the next day, the rich man acted as if it was the first time he was seeing the poet.

"I came to see you yesterday and read poems. You asked me to come to take the reward today", Raidas reminded.

"Oh yes! Look, you may be able to compose poetry, but you have no common sense. If I had wished to reward you, I would have given the gifts yesterday itself. I told you to come the next day as I did not want to hurt you. You came here unnecessarily", said the rich man.

Raidas was upset to hear this. But he could not do anything and had to leave. On his way home, he saw Birbal riding a horse.

"Raja Birbal! You are the right person to tell me what to do", Raidas called.

"Come to my house and tell me everything", Birbal said.

Raidas told Birbal all that had happened. "What the rich man has done was very wrong. He must be taught a good lesson. Tell me, do you have a close friend whom you can trust?" Birbal asked.

"Yes", Raidas replied.

"Then go to him. Give these 5 gold mohurs and ask him to arrange a grand feast on the coming night of the full moon. Tell him to invite the rich man to the feast. I shall tell you the other details of my plan later",

Birbal said and handed over 5 gold mohurs to Raidas.

Raidas accepted the gold mohurs and went to see his friend Mayadas. He told Mayadas all about Birbal's plan and gave him the 5 gold mohurs.

"Take this to arrange a lavish feast. Don't forget to invite the rich man to the feast", said Raidas.

Mayadas bought all the things he needed for the feast. Then he went to the rich man's house.

"I am giving a grand feast on the night of the full moon. You must come. My guests will be served on golden plates which I plan to gift to them later", said Mayadas.

The rich man accepted the invitation greedily. He waited for the night of the full moon eagerly. He dressed in rich clothes and wore costly jewels.

The rich man entered Mayadas' house. He found that not many people were there except for Mayadas and Raidas. They welcomed him and began talking.

The two friends went on talking for a long time. They had actually eaten their food before the rich man arrived. So, they were not hungry.

Hours passed. The rich man felt very hungry. He had not eaten much that day as he wanted to have a good time at the feast. When it was nearing midnight, he could wait no longer.

"I am feeling hungry. When will dinner be served?" he asked.

"Dinner...? What dinner?" Mayadas asked.

"But you invited me to a feast tonight", the rich man protested.

"Do you have any proof?" asked Raidas.

The rich man had no answer to that question.

"Even if we say that we invited you to a dinner, it was just to please you and we don't like to hurt others", Mayadas added.

Just then Birbal entered the house.

"Do you remember that you said the same thing to Raidas when he read his poems to you?" he asked.

"I am sorry for my mean act, Raidas. You are a good poet and deserve to be rewarded. Take this pearl necklace as a gift from me", said the rich man and removed his necklace and gave it to Raidas.

Birbal was glad that he had seen that poetic justice was done.

❋❋ ❋❋ ❋❋

6. THE REUNION

Once Birbal was banished from the court by Akbar. Birbal went to live in a village where no one knew him. However, Akbar was soon sorry for his decision in sending Birbal away. He missed his intelligent conversation greatly. Akbar sent soldiers to find out where Birbal had gone, but none of them succeeded.

One day, a soldier told Akbar that a holy man and his two disciples wanted to see him.

"The disciples claim that their master is the wisest man on earth", said the soldier.

"Let them come in", Akbar said. He wanted the company of a wise man.

The holy man and his two disciples entered the court.

"O holy man, your disciples say that you are the wisest man on earth. My Ministers will ask you some questions. If you answer them satisfactorily, I will make you my Minister. But if you fail to answer them, you will be punished severely", Akbar said.

"My disciples have praised me greatly. But I am ready to face the rest", the holy man said.

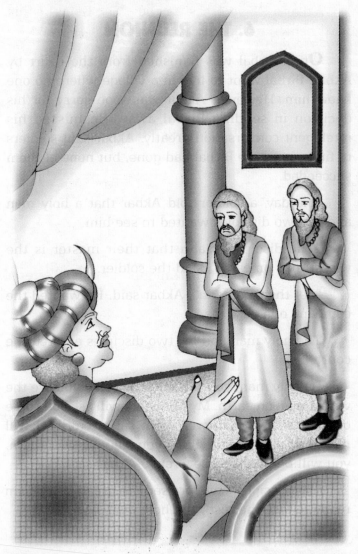

Akbar's "Navaratnas" or the "Nine Gems" of his court began to ask questions.

"Who is man's best friend in the world?" asked Raja Todarmal.

"His good sense", replied the holy man.

"Which is the most superior thing on earth?" asked Faizi.

"Knowledge", was the answer.

"Which is the shallowest pit in the world?" asked Abul Fazl.

"A woman's heart."

"What is that which cannot be recovered after it is lost?" asked Aziz Koka.

"Life."

"How far does the world extend?" asked Rahim Khan-i-Khan.

"Till one's death."

"What travels quicker than wind?" Raja Mansingh questioned.

"Man's imagination."

"What is the sweetest thing in the world?" Bhagwan Das put in.

"A baby's smile."

"Tansen, ask the holy man two questions", said Akbar.

"What is undying about music?" asked Tansen.

"The notes", replied the holy man at once.

Tansen's second question was : "What sounds sweetest at night?"

"Prayer to God", was the holy man's answer.

Now the Emperor himself decided to ask a couple of questions.

"What is most needed to rule over a Kingdom?" he asked.

"Diplomacy."

"What is the greatest enemy of a King?" Akbar wanted to know.

"His selfishness", the holy man said promptly.

Akbar was pleased with the holy man's replies. He thought that this would be a good opportunity to use the holy man for his personal benefit too.

"I am pleased to hear your sensible replies. But there is one thing I want to ask: can you perform any miracle?" he asked.

"Certainly! I can make the person you are thinking about to appear this very minute!" said the holy man.

"Right! Then bring my best friend Birbal here!" Akbar said.

The holy man did not utter a word. He simply removed his false beard and his wig. Akbar exclaimed with pleasant surprise.

"Birbal! I am glad to have you back. I should have known from the replies that it was you all the time!"

❋❋   ❋❋   ❋❋

7. AKBAR'S DREAM

One night, the Emperor Akbar had a strange dream. He woke up worried next morning. For he had dreamed that he had lost all except one of his teeth.

Akbar summoned the court astrologer and told him about his dream.

"What can my dream mean? Tell me at once!" he demanded.

The astrologer looked grave when he heard all the details.

"O Emperor! I am sorry to tell you that your dream means that all your relatives will die before you", he said.

Akbar did not like the astrologer's remark. So, he did not reward him. When Birbal came to court later that morning, Akbar narrated his dream.

"Can you tell me what my dream means, Birbal?" Akbar asked.

Birbal thought for a while.

"O Badshah! Your dream tells me that you will live longer than your relatives!" he explained.

Akbar was pleased with the way Birbal had explained that dream and rewarded him.

✳   ✳   ✳

8. BIRBAL'S CLEVERNESS

One day, a "sadhu" came to Akbar's court.

"O Badshah! I have heard that you have a collection of wise men, the 'Nine Gems' as your courtiers. Now, I want to test them. If at least one succeeds in answering my question, I shall bless this great Moghul Empire. Otherwise, be prepared to face bad times", the 'Sadhu' challenged.

"Should we take up the 'sadhu's' challenge?" Akbar and the other courtiers wondered nervously.

Birbal rose from his seat and said, "O Badshah! Let us take up the challenge of the 'sadhu', I shall answer his question."

The 'Sadhu' began talking.

"Once 3 travellers reached a Dharmasala or inn at night fall and asked the inn-keeper to give them each a room. The inn-keeper told them that he did not have 3 vacant rooms, but they could all stay in one room which had 3 cots. The travellers agreed. The inn-keeper told them that the rent of the room was 30 bronze coins which they gave at once.

Some time later, the man who kept the accounts came and told the inn-keeper that he had overcharged the travellers by 5 coins as the rent was really 25 bronze coins. The inn-keeper was an honest man.

He at once asked a servant to return the 5 coins to the travellers.

Now, the servant was not so honest. He thought that it was not possible to divide the 5 coins equally into 3 parts. So, how could he return equal amounts to the 3 travellers? Then he had an idea. He quietly put two coins into his pocket and gave one coin to each of the three travellers.

Here is the problem : there were 30 coins in all. 2 were taken by the servant and 27 coins were charged as rent. So, out of thirty coins, 27 were paid by the travellers and 2 were taken by the servant. But that means only 29 coins (27 + 2 = 29). Where did the thirtieth coin vanish?" - the 'sadhu' asked the court.

Although the problem seemed to be simple, the solution was hard to get. The courtiers calculated again and again but were still puzzled. At last they asked Birbal if he could answer.

"O holy man! You have asked a very easy question. You made it appear difficult by wording it so as to confuse everyone. According to the problem, the 3 travellers paid 30 coins and received 3 coins back. So, we think that they actually paid 27 coins and the accountant accepted 27 coins. But the answer is easy. Out of the 27 coins paid by the travellers, 2 were taken by the servant and the remaining 25 coins were the rent of the room. There is no missing coin. It is just a trick to fool the people! Is that right?" Birbal asked.

"Correct! well done, Birbal!" – the 'sadhu' praised. He turned to Akbar and said, "O Badshah! You will be remembered as the greatest Moghul Emperor and your Minister Birbal's fame will spread far and wide. My blessings to you all."

❈❈   ❈❈   ❈❈

9. THE BEST THING IN THE WORLD

The Emperor Akbar had many wives. One of them was a quarrelsome woman. Many people had complained to Akbar about her.

One day, she even spoke rudely to the Emperor himself. Akbar became very angry and decided to send her back to her mother's house.

"Get ready to go back to your mother's house at once!" - he shouted at her.

The Begum began weeping bitterly.

"I am sorry I was so rude! Please don't send me away" - she begged.

Akbar felt sorry for her. But he didn't change his decision.

"You can take what you like the most with you when you go", he said in a kinder tone.

The Begum knew that the Emperor would not relent. She wondered what to do. At last she remembered the wise Birbal. She wanted to ask him for help.

"But will he help me? I have said so many bad things about him", she thought with doubt.

However, she sent word to Birbal. He came to see her at once.

"O Birbal, I want your help badly. But I am feeling a little ashamed to ask you because I have said so many bad things about you", said Begum to Birbal.

"Never mind about all that! Please tell me what can I do for you", Birbal replied.

"The Emperor has decided to send me away to my mother's house forever. He told me that I can take whatever I like the best in this palace", said the Begum.

"I see!" Birbal replied. He thought for a minute and said, "This is what you should do ......" (he whispered in her ears).

The Begum looked happy when she heard Birbal's advice. Later that evening, she sent word to Emperor Akbar. He came to see her.

"I have packed my belongings. Please accept this 'sherbet' which I have made myself", she said and offered a glass to the Emperor.

Akbar was glad to see that the Begum looked calm. He drank the 'sherbet'. In a short while, he fell into a deep sleep.

The Begum at once summoned servants who placed the sleeping Emperor in a palanquin. Then she left for her mother's place.

The next day, Akbar woke up. He gazed at his strange surroundings. The Begum came in just then.

"Where am I?" he asked her.

"You are in the palace", she replied.

"But this is not my palace!" Akbar looked out of the window and said.

"O Badshah! you told me to take what I liked best when I went to my mother's house. So, I brought you whom I like best", she replied with a smile.

Akbar's anger vanished. He realised that no one other than Birbal could have advised Begum to do this.

❋❋ ❋❋ ❋❋

10. THE IMPOSSIBLE TASK

One day, the Emperor Akbar called Birbal to his palace.

"O Birbal, I want you to bring me a vessel of Ox's milk", he requested.

Birbal was startled by this unusual request, but he did not express it out.

"I shall get it for you, O Badshah! But I want a week's time", Birbal replied.

"All right", Akbar agreed and allowed Birbal to leave.

When it was evening, Birbal went home

"The Emperor has asked for a vessel of Ox's milk and has given me a week's time. But it is an impossible task. What shall I do?" Birbal thought with dismay.

Birbal's wife noted her husband's worried look and asked him what was wrong.

"The Emperor has asked me to get him in a week a vessel of Ox's milk. I don't know what to do", Birbal told her.

To his great surprise, his wife began laughing loudly.

"What an easy task! I'll tell you what to do later. But first promise me not to leave the house for six days", she said.

"I promise!" Birbal agreed at once. He knew that his clever wife would help him out of the tricky situation somehow.

Five days passed by. On the sixth night, Birbal's wife left her home with a large bundle of clothes and went to the palace. She opened the bundle near the lake and began washing them one by one.

The Emperor was awakened by the noise.

"Who is washing clothes in the lake?" he wondered and went to the balcony for a look. He sent his sentries to fetch the person.

"Why are you washing clothes so late at night?" he asked Birbal's wife.

"O Badshah! six days ago my husband gave birth to a baby. Our maid-servant did not come for work. So I have to do all the work myself. I just finished the other works before washing the clothes", she replied.

"What are you saying!" Akbar exclaimed. "How can a man give birth to a baby?"

The woman smiled at the Emperor.

"It is not surprising at all! If you can ask for Ox's milk, why can't a man give birth to a baby?" she asked.

Akbar nodded his head as he understood the truth in her statement. A man could not give birth to a baby, just as an Ox could not give milk. He remembered the impossible task he had asked Birbal to perform.

The Emperor rewarded Birbal's wife with gifts and sent her home.

❋❋   ❋❋   ❋❋